Maddy and Mia
TriPaw Tales

written by Pamela Adler

illustrated by Monique Seibel

To Sloan,
Be kind & believe in yourself!

Pamela Adler

&

BELLE ISLE BOOKS
www.belleislebooks.com

ISBN: 978-1-947860-79-7
LCCN: 2019920802

Project managed by Christina Kann

Printed in the United States of America

Published by
Belle Isle Books (an imprint of Brandylane Publishers, Inc.)
5 S. 1st Street
Richmond, Virginia 23219
belleislebooks.com | brandylanepublishers.com

BELLE ISLE BOOKS
www.belleislebooks.com

This book is dedicated to all God's creatures
who, by birth or circumstance, face
their seen and unseen challenges every day
with courage, perseverance, and hope.

To our amazing, real-life Mia:
Since the day we brought you home,
you have been an inspiration to us all.
My hope is that this book will encourage
children to follow your example—
to live courageously and believe in themselves.
The joy you have brought into my life is beyond measure.

Contents

The New Puppy

Maddy could barely contain her excitement as she walked home from school. Her family's pet poodle, Lacey, was expecting puppies at any time. That morning, Maddy's mother had been certain they would be born by dinnertime. Mom and Dad had told Maddy she could keep a puppy, so she had spent the previous few weeks trying to decide on a name.

When Maddy opened the front door, Lacey was not there to greet her as usual. As Maddy walked toward the spare bedroom, her mother met her in the hall with a big smile.

"Lacey had her puppies. They're all sleeping right now, so we must be very quiet and not disturb them," Mom said.

Maddy nodded and tiptoed into the room. As she peeked into the puppy pen Dad had built, she counted the tiny, sleeping puppies as they snuggled up to Lacey's tummy. One, two, three.

"Mommy, only three puppies?" Maddy whispered.

"Look closer," Mom said.

Maddy got down on her knees and gently petted Lacey's head. As she leaned over, Maddy saw a fourth, very small puppy trying to push its way up to Lacey's tummy. It was smaller than all the other puppies and struggling to climb up.

"Mommy, I see a very tiny one!" Maddy said.

"Yes, dear," Mom replied. "The smallest puppy in a litter is called a *runt*." Mom knelt down bedside Maddy. "Runts have a much harder time growing up because of their size. Sometimes the larger pups won't share their food, or they might push the runt away. This little girl will need extra help and attention as she grows up."

As Maddy watched, the runt crawled up to Lacey and began to nurse. Maddy could see it was very difficult for the tiny puppy to move.

"Mommy, why is it so hard for the runt to move around?"

Mom took hold of Maddy's hand. "This puppy's not only small; she only has three legs. She was born that way."

Maddy looked down at the small, helpless puppy sleeping next to Lacey. In that moment, Maddy knew in her heart that the runt was meant to be her one-of-a-kind companion. A tear rolled down Maddy's cheek as she squeezed her mother's hand and softly said, "I want to keep the runt because she's special."

Mom smiled and gave Maddy a hug. "I think this puppy will be a wonderful pet for you. Your next step is to decide on a name for her."

When Maddy went to bed that night, she could hardly wait for morning to come so she could cuddle with her new puppy and give her a special name.

After Maddy woke up the next morning, she walked quietly to the spare room, where Lacey was resting with her puppies. She sat down and gently petted Lacey on the head. Lacey wagged her tail in reply. "You're a good mom, Lacey," Maddy whispered with a smile. "Your babies are very cute!"

Maddy watched as the puppies woke up. As they squeaked and wriggled around the pen, Maddy spotted the runt in the corner, struggling to get up.

"Hi, little puppy-girl," Maddy said softly. "Let me help you!" Maddy reached into the pen and gently picked up her puppy. She carefully kissed the little girl on the head, then placed her next to Lacey. "We need to pick a better name for you than *runt* or *puppy-girl!*" Maddy said with a giggle.

Dad walked in with a cup of coffee in one hand and Lacey's bowl in the other. He set the bowl on the floor and gave Lacey a pat on the head as she started to eat her breakfast. "Did you decide on a name yet for your little tripod?" he asked.

Maddy turned to her dad with a puzzled look. "Tripod? What does that mean, Daddy?"

Dad quietly pulled up a chair next to Maddy and sat. "'Tripod' is an old Greek word that means 'three legs.' When your puppy gets a little older and starts to walk, she won't do it like the other puppies. She'll have to hop on her one front leg. If anyone asks why she hops, you can tell them it's because she's a tripod."

As Maddy gazed down at her puppy, her heart swelled with love. "She is a brave and strong little girl. I love her so much, and I promise I will always take care of her."

Dad smiled and said, "I'm very proud of you, Maddy." He paused, sipping his coffee, then asked, "So, what's her name?"

"I like the name Mia," Maddy replied. "It's a tiny name for my tiny puppy."

Dad stood up and said, "That sounds like a perfect name for her. From now on, we'll call her Maddy's little Mia!"

Maddy clapped her hands with delight. She reached into the pen and picked up her puppy. "My Mia!" she whispered. "You are my special little tripod, and I promise to take care of you forever." Then Maddy carefully wrapped Mia in a cozy blanket and rocked her to sleep.

A Trip to the Doctor

Maddy opened her sleepy eyes and saw sunlight shining brightly through her bedroom window. As she climbed out of bed, she saw that Mia was still snoozing on her puppy pillow in the warm sun.

"Good morning, Mia!" Maddy said. "Guess what? You are six months old today!"

Mia replied with a big yawn and a sleepy wag of her tail.

"Sometimes I miss your brothers and sister, but I know they are in good homes and loved very much."

Maddy put on her robe and slippers, smiling as she smelled the wonderful breakfast her mother was cooking. She picked up Mia and walked to the kitchen.

Mom had placed breakfast on the table, and Mia's morning snack was in her bowl.

"Morning, Mommy," Maddy said, covering her mouth as she yawned through her words.

"Breakfast is ready, you two sleepyheads," said Mom with a grin.

Maddy gave Mia a kiss and gently placed her next to her bowl. Mia eagerly ate her snack, and Maddy sat down at the table. As Maddy began to eat her breakfast, she felt a sharp pain in her ear.

"Mommy, my ear hurts," said Maddy with a frown. When she took another bite, it hurt again.

Mom walked over to Maddy and looked closely at her ear. "I don't see anything, but I think we should take you to the doctor and have him look *inside* your ear," said Mom.

At the doctor's office, a friendly nurse instructed Maddy to sit on a large, padded table. Mom sat in a chair next to Maddy with Mia in her lap. Strange and interesting things were all around the room. Jars of cotton balls and bottles of brightly colored liquids sat on the countertop. Maddy's eyes grew big when she saw a large diagram of an ear hanging on the wall.

"Mommy, would it be okay if Mia sat in my lap?" Maddy asked nervously.

"Of course, if you think she'll help you feel better," Mom replied.

Maddy nodded vigorously as her mother gently placed Mia in her lap. Maddy hugged Mia close, and Mia responded with a soft lick on Maddy's hand.

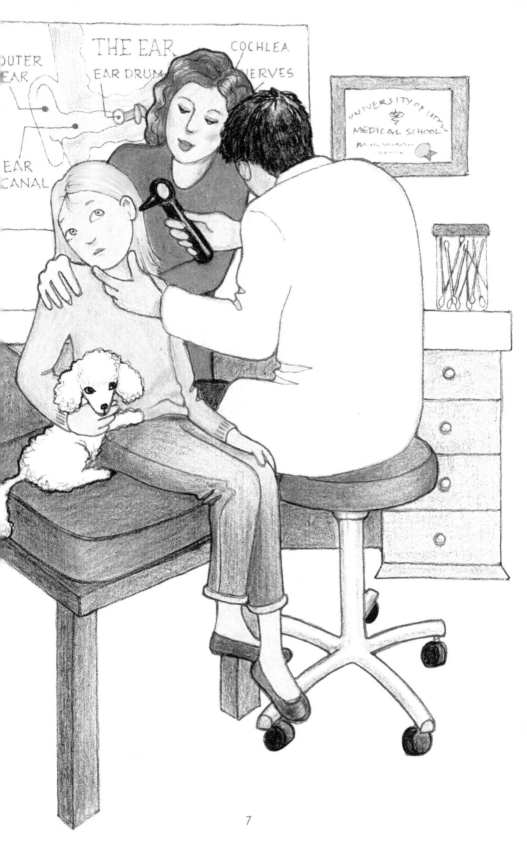

Soon, the doctor came into the room and sat down next to Maddy.

"Good morning, Maddy," he said in a friendly voice. "I'm Dr. Martinez. I understand you have an earache. Can you point to which one hurts for me?"

Maddy pointed to her painful ear and softly replied, "This one."

Dr. Martinez opened a drawer and pulled out a special instrument. "This is my ear flashlight," he explained. "It has batteries just like a regular flashlight, but on the end, there is a plastic ice cream cone. The cone lets me gently look inside your ear canal so I can see why it hurts." He pointed at the diagram on the wall to show Maddy where he was going to look.

Dr. Martinez let Maddy hold the ear flashlight and shine the light on her hand. Mia saw the light on Maddy's hand and let out a tiny squeak.

"It's okay, Mia. It doesn't hurt," said Maddy with a faint giggle. She gave Mia a pat on her head, then handed the instrument back to the doctor.

Mom held Maddy's hand, and the doctor carefully placed the cone into Maddy's ear. Mia let out another tiny squeak. Dr. Martinez smiled, peering through his instrument, and said, "Your little dog is watching us very closely."

"Mia is my very special dog," Maddy replied. "She is a tripod, but she can run very fast. She goes everywhere with me except to school."

Dr. Martinez smiled again. "Sounds like Mia is a brave little girl. And so are you, Maddy. I can see why your ear is hurting. You have an ear infection, and I know just what to do to fix it." The doctor removed the cone from Maddy's ear and patted her on the shoulder. "You're a very good patient, and only my best patients get one of *these*." The doctor pulled a red lollipop from his pocket and handed it to Maddy.

"Thank you very much!" Maddy said with a big sigh and a bigger smile.

When they returned home, Maddy took her medicine and then walked with Mia outside onto the grass. Suddenly Mia yelped and began to cry. "Daddy, come quick! Something is wrong with Mia!" shouted Maddy as she carried Mia inside.

Carefully, Maddy and her father searched Mia for whatever was hurting her. They soon discovered a large thorn stuck in Mia's paw. "My poor little Mia! Can you fix it, Daddy?" asked Maddy, choking back tears.

"I think we should take Mia to the veterinarian. He can take the thorn out faster and easier than I can," Dad replied.

Maddy carried Mia to the car, and they quickly drove to the vet's office.

As they waited for Dr. Sterling to look at Mia's paw, Maddy held her dog close and whispered, "Don't be afraid, Mia. I'll stay with you. This doctor will make your paw all better, just like my doctor did for my ear." Mia looked at Maddy and responded with another small lick on Maddy's hand.

Dr. Sterling came into the room, examined Mia's paw very slowly, and explained how he was going to remove the thorn. While Maddy held Mia very still, the vet placed a few drops of medicine on Mia's paw, then carefully pulled the sharp thorn out.

"All finished," said Dr. Sterling. "Mia's paw will be sore for a few days. Because she's a tripod, you might need to carry her a little more than you normally do until it heals, but she'll be fine." Maddy understood the doctor and felt very relieved that Mia was not seriously hurt.

"Mia was a very good patient today," said Dr. Sterling. "Maddy, do you think she'd like a treat?"

"Yes, I think she'd like that very much!" Maddy answered with a big smile. Dr. Sterling reached into his pocket and pulled out a doggie treat. "Look, Mia, your doctor has doggie treats in his pocket, just like my doctor has people treats!" said Maddy with a laugh.

Mia's tail wagged happily as Dr. Sterling held out the treat for her to sniff. Mia gently took the treat from the doctor's hand and eagerly ate it. Maddy and Dad thanked the vet for his help and left.

When they got home, Maddy told her mother about the trip to the veterinarian's office. They were all glad that Mia's paw would be better in a few days.

"That's very good news," Mom said. "You both were very good patients today. I think a cookie for each of you would make you feel even better."

"I think so, too!" exclaimed Maddy with big smile. She turned to Mia and asked, "Would you like a cookie, Mia?" Mia responded with a hearty bark, as if to say *yes!*

"You were so brave today, my little Mia. I love you so much!" said Maddy as they snuggled together in a soft chair and enjoyed their cookies.

A New Friend

It was a cool, cloudy day, and Maddy was happy to be inside her cozy room. As she sat at her desk, reading a book, Mia lay quietly on Maddy's bed.

"I'm almost done with my book," Maddy said as she turned to Mia. "We can go for a walk soon if it's not raining." Mia lifted her head and wagged her tail.

Dad came into Maddy's room with a raincoat on and Maddy's umbrella tucked under his arm. "Did you notice that the new neighbors are moving in across the street?" he asked.

Maddy jumped to her feet and rushed to look out her window. "Yes, I see them!" she exclaimed.

"I saw a young boy playing in the front yard a while ago," Dad continued. "He looks like he might be your age."

"Do you think it would be all right if I walked over to say hello?" Maddy asked.

"I think that's an excellent idea," Dad replied. "In fact, I think it would be a good idea for all of us to introduce ourselves. Mom is making some cookies to take along."

"Oh boy, let's go!" Maddy exclaimed as she scooped Mia into her arms. "You can come, too, my Mia!"

As Maddy walked into the kitchen, Mom was placing warm cookies onto a plate. With Lacey on her leash and Mia tucked under Maddy's arm, the family walked across the street to meet their new neighbors.

"Hello! Welcome to the neighborhood," said Dad as they walked up the driveway. "I'm Greg Attwood. This is my wife, Rachel, and our daughter, Maddy."

"We're the Baldwins," said Mr. Baldwin as they all shook hands. "It's very nice of you to come over."

As the adults talked, Maddy saw a young boy ride up the driveway on his bicycle. When he got near, he got off his bike, then walked up to meet them.

"Hi. My name is Finn," he said in a quiet voice. When Finn saw Mia in Maddy's arms, his face broke into a big smile. "What's your dog's name?"

"Her name is Mia," Maddy replied with a smile. "And my name is Maddy. Would you like a cookie? My mom just made them."

Finn nodded. "Yes, please!"

Maddy carefully took the plate of cookies from her mother and held it out to Finn. He picked one and eagerly took a bite.

Maddy did the same, and as they chewed their cookies, they began to laugh.

"These are my favorite kind of cookie," said Finn.

"Mine too!" replied Maddy. "I like them even better with a glass of milk."

Finn nodded, then turned to his mother and asked, "Mom, can Maddy and I go inside and have some milk with our cookies?"

"Of course, honey," Mrs. Baldwin answered.

As Maddy, Mia, and Finn walked toward the house, they could hear the parents talking about the school that Finn would be attending in a few days.

When they sat down to enjoy their cookies and milk, Maddy noticed Finn was frowning.

"What's wrong?" she asked.

Finn shrugged. "I guess I'm a little nervous about going to a new school."

"Don't worry!" said Maddy. "I have lots of friends there, and they're all really fun. The teachers are very nice, and the playground has lots of fun stuff to do. My mom walks with me to school every day. You can walk with us if you'd like."

"That sounds great—thanks," Finn said, looking relieved. "What's your favorite thing on the playground? I like the swings."

"I like the jungle gym," replied Maddy, and they both laughed.

Mia stood up in Maddy's lap, barked a tiny bark, and wagged her tail.

"What is it, Mia?" Maddy asked. She looked in the same direction as Mia and saw a large orange cat slowly stroll into the kitchen.

"Oh, my gosh, you have a cat!" exclaimed Maddy. She tightened her arm around Mia.

Finn grinned. "That's Zoey. We adopted her from the animal shelter a year ago. She's friendly with everyone, and she loves to sit in my lap."

Maddy and Mia watched as Zoey jumped from the floor into Finn's lap, and then turned to look at Mia. Maddy took a deep breath and whispered to Finn, "Mia has never met a cat before. I hope they won't fight."

Mia's tail continued to wag as she leaned closer to the cat. Zoey stretched out toward Mia, her tail flicking. Finn and Maddy held their breaths as the two pets got close enough to sniff each other's noses.

"Zoey, these are our new neighbors, Maddy and Mia," said Finn calmly.

Maddy said, "Mia, this is our new neighbor Finn and his cat, Zoey."

Mia sat back down in Maddy's lap, and Zoey purred as Finn scratched her chin. Maddy and Finn looked at each other and nodded with sighs of relief.

"This will be so much fun! Any time we want to play together, Zoey and Mia can play too!" exclaimed Maddy.

Finn laughed and said, "Yeah, I think you're right!"

As Mia and Zoey snoozed on their owners' laps, Maddy and Finn finished their milk and cookies. They talked about walking together to school and all the fun they were going to have being neighbors.

The Golden Rule

Saturday was Maddy's favorite day of the week, and after lunch was her favorite time *on* Saturday. As Maddy eagerly slipped on her play shoes, she couldn't help but smile. It was time to walk to the park!

"Come here, my Mia," said Maddy. "I need to put your harness on for our walk."

Mia jumped up and hopped over to Maddy. Maddy placed the harness over Mia's head and locked it in place around her chest. Maddy giggled as she watched Mia's tail wag happily.

"Are you ready to go, Maddy?" Mom called.

"Yes, Mommy, we are," replied Maddy. She picked up Mia, and they headed outside with Mom and Lacey.

The park was a short walk from their house, and Maddy enjoyed looking at the flowers and shady trees along the way. As they turned the last corner and entered the park, Maddy saw some of her school friends on the playground. Mom leaned over and asked, "Isn't that Finn over there playing on the swings?"

"Yes!" Maddy answered with a big smile. "Mom, will you watch Mia while I play with Finn?"

"Of course. We'll be sitting on the bench by the drinking fountain," Mom replied.

Maddy thanked her mother and dashed across the grass to join Finn. When Finn saw Maddy running toward him, he smiled and waved. Maddy waved back, then eagerly sat in the vacant swing Finn was holding out for her.

"Hi!" Maddy said, a bit out of breath. "Thanks for saving a swing for me."

"Sure thing," Finn replied.

As the two friends talked and laughed, Maddy noticed a girl sitting all alone on the edge of the sandbox.

"Finn, do you know who that is?" Maddy asked.

"I've seen her a few times at school, but I don't know her name," Finn said. "I think she's one grade lower than us. I saw those mean kids talking to her a while ago," he added, looking across the playground. Maddy looked over and saw three boys sitting at a table, laughing and pointing at some of the other kids.

Maddy frowned. "I've seen those boys here before. They like to tease the younger kids. They think it's funny to make other people feel bad."

Finn nodded. "They're bullies."

Maddy and Finn jumped off their swings and walked over to the sandbox. As they got closer, the girl raised her head to see who was coming. When Maddy smiled at her, she smiled back.

"Hi. I'm Maddy, and this is Finn. We noticed you're sitting all by yourself. Would you like to come play with us on the swings?"

The girl slowly nodded and answered, "Okay."

Finn could see she was very shy. "What's your name?" he asked.

"Hannah," she replied as she peeked over her glasses.

Finn smiled and said, "Okay, Hannah, the swings are this way. Follow me!"

As the three friends walked toward the swings, Hannah told Maddy, "I don't want to walk near those mean boys. They made fun of my glasses."

Maddy nodded and said, "One time, they made fun of Finn's freckles. They're mean bullies, and we don't want to go near them, either."

Hannah was glad to have Maddy and Finn to play with. Soon she was laughing, and she forgot all about what the mean kids had said to her.

After a while, Mom walked over and told Maddy it was time to go home.

Maddy turned to Hannah and said, "Would you like to meet here next Saturday and play?"

Hannah smiled and said, "Yes, I would!"

The following Saturday, Finn and Maddy walked to the park together. As they entered the park, they saw Hannah on the swings. Maddy and Finn ran up to her, and soon the three friends were laughing and pumping hard to see who could swing the highest. Maddy looked toward the big slide and noticed a boy sitting at the bottom. His hands were in his jacket pockets, and his head was slumped down as he shifted his feet.

"Look over there," Maddy said. "Isn't that one of the mean kids we saw here last week?"

Hannah and Finn looked toward the slide.

"Sure is," replied Hannah with a scowl. "He's the one who said mean things about my glasses."

"He's the one who made fun of my freckles," added Finn.

Maddy stopped swinging and said, "I wonder where his friends are."

Finn and Hannah stopped swinging too, and they looked around. The other mean boys were sitting at the same table as before. They pointed and laughed at the boy on the slide.

Hannah turned to Maddy and said, "I wonder why they're doing that."

"I don't know," replied Maddy. "But he looks sad and all alone, like you did last Saturday."

Hannah looked at Finn and Maddy and slowly said, "I think we should walk over and see if he's okay. But I don't want to go by myself."

Finn took a step forward and cleared his throat. "I don't blame you. Let's all go."

The three friends walked cautiously toward the slide. The boy was wearing a baseball cap. As they got closer, they could see he had a swollen lip.

Finn took a deep breath and gathered up his courage. "We noticed you were sitting here all by yourself. Would you like to play on the swings with us?"

The boy kept his head down and pulled his cap lower over his face. He didn't answer Finn. They all could hear the mean boys laughing over at their table.

Hannah nervously stepped a little closer. "Did you fall down and get hurt?" she asked. "Do you want us to get a grown-up to help you?"

The boy shook his head. "I'm okay. I fell off my bike after school yesterday, and I got a little banged up." He lifted his head to show Maddy, Finn, and Hannah his swollen lip and bruised nose. "When I fell, I hit my nose and mouth pretty hard on the handlebars. I knocked three teeth loose. Now I have to wear these ugly braces." He gave the three friends a timid smile to show them the shiny metal braces on his teeth.

Suddenly Maddy realized that the mean boys were making fun of him, just as he had done in the past to Hannah and Finn. She plopped down in the sand next to the boy and said, "My name is Maddy. And this is Hannah and Finn. What's your name?"

"Jack," he replied.

Hannah sat on Jack's other side and peeked under the brim of his cap. "Those mean boys are teasing you about your braces, aren't they?"

Jack nodded. "And about falling off my bike."

Finn sat down next to Hannah and turned to Jack. "It doesn't feel very good, does it?" he asked.

Jack dropped his head down again and softly said, "No, it sure doesn't. The dentist said I have to wear the braces until my teeth are strong again. I can't help it."

Hannah quickly spoke up. "Just like I can't help it that I need to wear glasses so I can see better. And Finn has freckles from playing in the sun."

Maddy rested her hand on Jack's shoulder. "Everyone is different. I have a dog named Mia, and she was born with only three legs. I love her with all my heart, just the way she is, even though she looks different from other dogs. Being different is what makes her so special; just like Hannah is different because of her glasses, and Finn is different because of his freckles. Now you know how they felt when you made fun of them. Bullying anybody for any reason is wrong. My mom always says it's a good rule to treat everyone the same way you want to be treated."

Jack turned to Hannah and Finn. "I'm really sorry about teasing you. I didn't understand how it hurt your feelings until now. I was wrong, and I promise I'll never do it again."

Finn and Hannah looked at each other and smiled. "What about your laughing friends over there?" asked Finn.

Jack stood up and said in a firm voice, "They're not my friends anymore. And if I see them bullying anyone again, I'll do what I can to stop them."

The friends stood up. Finn said, "Good job, Jack!" Maddy nodded in agreement, and Hannah gave Jack a high-five.

As Maddy, Hannah, and Finn started walking toward the jungle gym, Jack turned to start walking home.

Hannah said, "Jack, where are you going? Don't you want to play on the jungle gym with us?"

Jack turned to Hannah with a puzzled look. "Me? You want to be friends with me?"

Finn laughed. "Sure! We don't care if you have braces! Come on. I'll race you!"

As Jack and Finn ran toward the jungle gym, Hannah and Maddy walked together. "It'll be fun to have another friend to play with," said Hannah with a smile.

"It sure will!" replied Maddy, and the girls ran to catch up with Finn and Jack.

Courage and Kindness

Birthday parties are fun occasions to share with friends. Maddy had been looking forward to her friend Amber's pizza party ever since the invitation arrived two weeks earlier.

"This is going to be such a fun day, my Mia! And guess what?" Maddy said excitedly. "You get to come with me! I get to see my friend Amber, eat pizza, and hold you in my lap all at the same time!"

Mia cocked her head to the side as if trying to understand what Maddy was telling her. Maddy laughed out loud.

"My Mia, you're so funny!"

Maddy finished changing her clothes, then carried Mia to the kitchen. Mom was wrapping the birthday gift in pretty flowered paper.

"Let's go, Maddy!" Dad called from the garage.

"Coming, Daddy!" Maddy replied. "Thank you, Mommy. It looks perfect." Maddy took the gift from her mother and tucked Mia under her arm, and soon they were on their way to the party.

As Maddy and Dad arrived, they saw lots of children playing games and running around the playground outside the pizza parlor. Lots of colored balloons were tied to the picnic tables, and one table had a big cake sitting in the middle. As Maddy looked around for Amber, she noticed a young boy being helped out of a car and into a wheelchair.

"I've never seen him before," said Maddy to her father. "I wonder what happened to him."

Dad said, "People use wheelchairs for many different reasons. Sometimes they've been in an accident, or they have a disease that prevents them from walking. Sometimes they're in a wheelchair for a short time, and sometimes it's for their whole life. A wheelchair helps people move around when their legs don't work like yours or mine." Dad paused and then added, "I think that boy is very brave to come here today, don't you?"

Maddy nodded as she watched the boy turn the wheels of his wheelchair to push himself up the path toward the play area.

Maddy got out of the car with Mia and made her way to the picnic tables. She placed her gift next to the others. As she turned around, she saw Amber running toward her.

"Hi, Maddy! Hi, Mia!" Amber said excitedly. "I'm so glad you came to my party!"

"Me, too! Happy birthday!" Maddy replied as they hugged.

"Thanks. You're just in time for pizza," said Amber. "Will you and Mia sit next to me?"

Maddy smiled. "Sure we will. Won't we, Mia?" Mia wagged her tail and licked Maddy on the hand.

As Maddy followed Amber, she noticed Jack and Finn talking to Hannah at the cake table. A short distance behind them, the boy in the wheelchair sat alone against the pizza parlor's wall in the shade. As the rest of the children took their seats, the boy began to push himself toward a table as well.

"Who's that boy in the wheelchair?" Maddy asked Amber.

"That's my neighbor, Jason," Amber replied.

As Maddy sat down, she noticed Jason struggling with his wheelchair. One of the front wheels was stuck in a wide crack in the cement. Jason pushed and pulled on the hand grips, but his chair would not budge. Maddy looked around for an adult, but they were all busy bringing out the pizzas and carrying pitchers of soda.

With Mia in her arms, Maddy quickly walked over to see if Jason needed help. "It looks like you're stuck. Need some help?" she asked.

Jason lifted his head and saw Mia looking at him. A big smile spread across his face. "Yes, please. That would be great," he answered. "I'm Jason."

Maddy smiled in return. "I'm Maddy, and this is my dog Mia. What can we do to get your wheel out?"

Jason scratched his head and frowned at the deep crack gripping his front wheel. "I think if you push really hard from the back and I steer toward the tables, it will come out."

Maddy took a deep breath. "Okay. But I need you to hold Mia in your lap so I can use both hands."

As Maddy gently placed Mia in Jason's lap, Jason noticed Mia was missing a front leg.

"I don't mean to be nosy, but why does Mia only have three legs?" Jason asked.

Maddy looked lovingly at Mia and said, "She was born that way."

Jason lifted Mia close to his face and whispered softly, "I know how you feel, Mia. I was born with both my legs, but they don't work, so I use a wheelchair. You were born with just three legs, but you can hop. We get around just fine anyway, don't we?" Mia wagged her tail, and Jason chuckled as he gave her a hug.

Maddy remembered what her father had told her in the car. She thought Jason was the most courageous person she'd ever met.

Jason turned to Maddy and said, "The pizza is getting cold! Are you ready to do this, Maddy?"

Maddy walked around to the back of the wheelchair and grabbed the handles. "Okay, Jason, hold on tight to Mia. One, two, three, PUSH!"

With the force of their combined pushes, the wheel popped out of the crack, and suddenly Jason's wheelchair raced toward the tables!

"Oh, my gosh!" shouted Maddy.

"Whoa, slow down!" shouted Jason, wide-eyed as he tried to apply the brakes.

"Arf!" barked Mia. "Arf! Arf!"

Over at the tables, other children heard Mia barking and

jumped up to help. Amber dashed over to Maddy and grabbed one handle on the back of the wheelchair, and Maddy moved over to use both hands on the other handle. Together, the girls pulled hard, and the chair began to slow down. Finn and Jack stood shoulder-to-shoulder and stretched their arms out to catch Jason and Mia before they could crash into the table.

"Jason, don't let Mia fall out!" shouted Maddy.

Jason nodded and wrapped both arms around Mia. When Jason approached the table, Finn and Jack each grabbed an armrest, and the wheelchair finally came to a stop.

After making sure Jason and Mia were all right, Amber guided them to the nearest table and stationed Jason at the end. Maddy walked around to face Jason, and they began to laugh.

"That was kind of scary, but we did it!" Maddy exclaimed, panting.

"We sure did!" Jason replied. "Thanks a lot for helping me, Maddy." Mia barked and licked Jason's hand. "And thank you, too, brave little Mia!" he added with a big smile. "I think you had fun going for a fast ride with me."

Maddy giggled as she picked Mia up from Jason's lap. "I think she did, too!"

Once Amber's dad and the other adults made sure nobody was hurt, kids began to take their seats again. Jason turned to

Maddy and Amber and asked, "Will you sit next to me for pizza?"

Before Amber and Maddy could answer him, Mia barked a loud, happy bark that made them all laugh. Maddy turned to Jason and said, "That means YES!"

Everyone enjoyed the delicious pizza. And when Amber blew out her birthday candles, Jason cheered the loudest.

Give and Take

Maddy loved playing with her dolls. She had a special shelf in her bookcase for them to sit on. Each one had a name that Maddy had selected, and they all wore fancy, colorful dresses.

One day, Maddy decided to have a tea party with Mia and two of their favorite dolls. As Maddy carefully set out the cups and teapot on the small table under her window, Mia watched from her special chair.

"Who should have tea with us today, Mia?" asked Maddy as she stood in front of her bookcase. "Hmm, I think it's Molly and Abigail's turn." Maddy carefully placed the dolls in their chairs, then sat down next to Mia.

As Maddy poured the pretend tea (which was actually water) into each cup, she chatted with her dolls and warned Mia not to spill hers on the table. After a while, Maddy stopped playing and gazed out the window.

"I wish my dolls could talk and laugh with me," Maddy said to Mia with a sigh. "Our tea party would be much more fun."

Maddy saw Finn leaving his house and crossing the street toward her house. Maddy picked up Mia and dashed to the front door and opened it just as Finn got there.

"Hi, Finn!" Maddy said with a smile. "I saw you coming from my window."

"Hi," Finn replied. "My dad just brought home a new game for me. Would you like to come over to my house and play?"

Maddy asked her mother's permission to go, and soon the two friends were sitting on the floor in Finn's cozy kitchen. As Finn set up the game and read the rules aloud, Maddy noticed the game board had pictures of dragons, castles, and warriors with swords on it.

"I think this is a boy's game, Finn," said Maddy.

Finn paused and looked at Maddy. "Why do you say that?"

"The pictures and pieces all look like it's a game made for boys," said Maddy, pointing to the board.

Finn squinted at the board, then said, "So what? Does that mean you don't want to play?"

Maddy scrunched her nose and shook her head. "Not really."

Finn took a deep breath and looked Maddy in the eye. "It's a game that anyone can play. Before you decide you don't like it, you should try it. You might be surprised and have fun."

"I still think I'd rather play something else."

"Okay then," said Finn, throwing his hands up in frustration. "Since you won't play my game, you pick something to do instead."

Maddy pondered for a moment, then smiled. "I know. Let's have a tea party!"

Finn's mouth fell open. "Are you kidding? Boys don't go to tea parties!"

Maddy held up her hand. "Hold on!" she said, looking Finn straight in the eye, just as he had done to her. "Didn't you just tell me that before you decide you don't like something, you should try it? Have you ever been to a tea party?"

Finn shook his head. "I don't want to, either. Tea parties are silly, and they're for girls."

As the two friends sat across from each other in silence, Maddy suddenly had an idea. "Okay, Finn, I'll make you a deal. I'll play your game if you'll come to my tea party."

Finn was quiet for a moment, tapping his fingers on the game board, trying to decide. Finally, he replied, "Okay, deal."

Finn's cat, Zoey, sat nearby and watched as Finn quickly finished setting up the game. Soon, Maddy and Finn were having a great time playing together. Maddy pretended she was an elf warrior, and Finn was a poor farm boy. They had to use their wits and imagination to defeat the demons and giants guarding a

beautiful princess. It was an exciting game, and when it was over, Maddy helped Finn put it away.

Maddy said, "You were right. That was a fun game. It wasn't just for boys. Now it's time for the tea party at my house!"

Mom was in the kitchen when Maddy and Finn arrived.

"Mom, Finn and I are going to play tea party in my room," said Maddy. "Can you help me get it ready, please?"

Mom looked at Finn with raised eyebrows. Finn blushed as he cleared his throat and stared at the floor.

"Sure," Mom said with a grin. "I have some cookies and a special tea I think Finn will really like. Get your table and tea-cups ready, and I'll bring the goodies."

"Thanks, Mom," said Maddy.

With Mia happily leading the way, Finn quickly retreated to Maddy's room. He couldn't help but smile as he watched Maddy place Mia in her chair.

"I usually have my dolls sit with me, but this time it can be just us," Maddy said.

Finn blushed again and replied, "That's fine with me," as he peered out the window.

Mom came in with the teapot and a plate of cookies. She set them on the table and gave Maddy a wink. "Here you go. Have fun, you two."

Maddy tried hard not to giggle.

Finn looked at the teapot and asked Maddy, "What's in there?"

"Tea, silly. It's a tea party."

Finn squinted his eyes and said, "Um, I'll just have cookies."

Maddy shook her head. "We have a deal, remember?" She passed the cookies to Finn and poured the tea into each of their cups. Maddy picked up her cup and said, "Come on, take a sip."

Finn reluctantly picked up his cup. As he went to sip the tea, he peered inside the cup and stopped. Puzzled, he looked at Maddy. "This isn't tea," exclaimed Finn. "It's chocolate milk!"

Maddy began to laugh so hard she nearly spilled her milk. Finn began to laugh as well, and then he eagerly gulped down the cold chocolate milk. Together, they finished the plate of cookies and had another cup of "tea" while they talked about school.

Finn shared a very tiny piece of his last cookie with Mia, then turned to Maddy. "You were right. Tea parties can be fun, and they aren't always just for girls. Especially when they include chocolate milk!"

Maddy giggled. "I'm glad we each got to try something new and fun today. Maybe we can do it again some time."

Finn agreed, and the two friends ran outside to play.

The Surprise

The hot summer sun was already warming the patio when Maddy and Mia stepped outside to water the garden. Mia hopped over to the cool, soft grass and stretched out under a shady tree.

"Good girl, my Mia," Maddy said. "You stay there while I water Mommy's flowers and vegetables."

Maddy turned on the hose and smiled as the cold water poured onto the patio and puddled under her bare feet. Suddenly, Mia appeared and barked at the water.

"Don't be afraid, Mia. The water won't hurt you," Maddy explained.

She put a tiny amount of water in her hand and offered it to Mia. Mia took a taste, then ran through the puddle. She barked at the fast-moving water coming from the hose and tried to drink some. Soon, Mia's paws and ears were dripping wet, but she didn't seem to mind—playing in the water wasn't scary. It was fun!

"My silly Mia!" Maddy said with a loud laugh. "I remember you were afraid of the water when you were a puppy. But you're a brave girl now!" Mia barked again and hopped back to the grass.

Dad walked outside through the sliding glass door. "When you're finished with watering, can you help me with something?" he asked.

"Okay, Daddy. I'm almost done," Maddy replied. She dried Mia off with a towel and walked to the kitchen to see her father.

Mom was sitting at the table. "Maddy," she said, "how would you feel about having a baby sister or brother?"

Maddy's eyes grew big. "Oh, Mom, I would love to have a sister!" Maddy ran to Mom and gave her a hug. Mom kissed Maddy on the cheek and smiled.

"We're glad to hear that," Dad said. "Mom is going to have a baby in a few months. We don't know if it's a brother or a sister, but Mom will need lots of help. The first thing we need to do is get the nursery ready. Can you help me with that today?"

Maddy clapped her hands and answered, "Yes, Daddy!"

Dad made a list of items the nursery needed. When he was finished, he said to Maddy, "We still have a lot of these things from when you were a baby. We have to go down to the basement to get them."

Maddy froze. The basement! She had always thought the basement was a scary place. It was dark and sometimes very cold. Maddy did not want to go down there!

"Come on, Maddy," Dad said as he unlocked the door to the basement. "You can help me carry up the boxes with the baby clothes."

Maddy swallowed hard. "I think I'll wait here," she said nervously as she clung tightly to Mia.

Dad grinned. "You're not still afraid of the basement, are you?" he asked.

Maddy nodded.

"Hmm," Dad replied. "I know you were afraid when you were little, but you're much older now."

"I know," Maddy answered in a small voice. Mia looked up at Maddy and gave her a soft lick on her hand. Maddy took a deep breath and said, "Will you hold my hand, Daddy?"

"Of course," Dad said.

With Mia tucked under her arm and Dad firmly holding her hand, Maddy started down the stairs, her heart racing. When they reached the bottom, Dad switched on another light. Maddy stood very still, gripping her father's hand as she looked all around the bright, tidy room.

"It looks different," she whispered. "It used to be dark and creepy."

Dad smiled. "Sometimes, when we go places or see things when we're young, they seem very big or scary. But when we grow

a little older and we see them again, they don't seem that way at all." He paused. "I used to be afraid of the attic in the house I grew up in. But when I got older, it became my favorite place to play." He gently squeezed Maddy's hand. "Ready to get those boxes with me?"

Mia gave Maddy another lick on her hand as if to say, *You can do it!* Maddy nodded and let go of Dad's hand. "If Mia is brave enough to play in the water, then I can be brave too." Maddy boldly stepped into the room.

It didn't take long for Maddy and Dad to carry up the boxes they needed for the nursery. Over the next few months, Maddy helped Mom organize the baby clothes and watched Dad hang colorful pictures all around the room.

When it was time for the baby to be born, Maddy's parents took Maddy and Mia to Finn's house. Maddy spent the day playing at the park and helping Finn and his father put a puzzle together. They were just finishing dinner when there was a knock at the door.

"Daddy!" Maddy exclaimed as her father entered the kitchen. She jumped into his arms and squeezed his neck tightly. "Did my sister come?" Finn and his parents stood nearby, waiting to hear the news.

"Yes, she did," Dad replied. "But I have a surprise for you. You also have a brother!"

Maddy's eyes grew big, and the kitchen became quiet. "Two babies?" she asked.

"That's right. Twins!" Dad said with a chuckle.

Maddy, Finn, and Finn's parents all began to laugh, and soon everyone was sharing hugs.

"When can I see them? When is Mommy coming home?" Maddy asked.

Dad explained that Mom and the babies needed to stay at the hospital for a few days to make sure they were all strong enough to come home.

Suddenly, Maddy stopped laughing and turned to her father. "I think this means we have to go back down to the basement to get more baby things."

Maddy's father grinned and said, "I think you're right. Maybe Finn would like to help us this time."

Maddy turned to Finn, but before she could ask, he was already speaking.

"The basement?" Finn took a step back. "I think I might be busy that day," he muttered, his voice trailing off. Maddy giggled.

"Don't be scared, Finn," said Maddy as she cuddled Mia in her arms. "Mia and I will go with you!" Mia agreed with a tiny bark, and Finn breathed a sigh of relief.

Dad thanked Finn and his parents for taking care of Maddy and Mia. He turned to Maddy and said, "Well, big sister, are you ready to go home?"

Maddy nodded. As Dad carried her and Mia home, Maddy knew that today was the happiest day she'd ever had!

Acknowledgments

I would like to acknowledge the people who supported and advised me as I traveled down this new and oftentimes bumpy path: my husband, George; my sons, Greg and Ryan; my dear friends Mona, Shirley, Vangie, and Janet; my awesome illustrator, Monique; my editor, Christina; and many other great friends who encouraged me to keep writing.

Thanks to all of you!

About the Author

 **Pamela Adler** was born in Oregon, but she moved to California as an infant with her parents and two older brothers. She grew up on the San Francisco peninsula and attended junior college until she met her future husband while working at a local movie theater. They married in 1975, and three years later, they started a family with the first of two sons. Pamela worked full time as a dental office manager for twenty-eight years and part-time as a magician's assistant. She retired in 2014. Pamela had the opportunity in 1998 to give an abandoned dog a forever home; from that day on, adopting rescued dogs and feral cats became her passion. *Maddy and Mia: TriPaw Tales* is her first book, inspired by her real-life tripod, Mia! Pamela lives in the San Francisco Bay Area with her husband of forty-four years, along with their pack of five rescue dogs and five feral cats.

About the Illustrator

 **Monique Seibel** has worked as an illustrator, graphic designer, copyeditor, writer, and calligrapher. After earning a degree in art, she spent a few years teaching, an experience that convinced her to return to her lifelong passion. She was lucky enough to combine art with what she calls her hobby—linguistics—in a job that called for graphic design as well as editing and writing. After twenty years in the tech world, Monique opened a calligraphy business, specializing in handwritten invitations and wedding program design. Now "retired," she continues to draw, paint, and volunteer her skills. She is an avid tennis player. *Maddy and Mia: TriPaw Tales* is the second children's book she has illustrated. As a mother and grandmother, Monique felt a connection with Maddy, and thanks to her own little Havanese bichon, with Mia as well. A native of New York who has also lived in the mid-Atlantic states and the Midwest, Monique and her husband have resided in the San Francisco Bay Area for many years.

CPSIA information can be obtained
at www.ICGtesting.com
Printed in the USA
BVHW020746100321
601558BV00005B/5